THE
KWEEKS
OF
KOOKATUMDEE

Bill Peet

Houghton Mifflin Company Boston

To Bill, Barbara, and Michael

Library of Congress Cataloging in Publication Data

Peet, Bill.
    The kweeks of Kookatumdee.

    Summary: The birdlike kweeks are starving because
their island does not have enough ploppolop fruit trees
to feed them all, until Quentin makes an amazing
discovery.
    1. Children's stories, American. [1. Islands—
Fiction. 2. Stories in rhyme] I. Title.
PZ8.3.P2764Kw   1985   [E]   84-22379
ISBN 0-395-37902-4

Printed in the United States of America

RNF ISBN 0-395-37902-4
PAP ISBN 0-395-48656-4

WOZ 10 9 8 7 6

Far off somewhere in the Tumbuzzaroo sea,
On the jungle island of Kookatumdee,
There once lived a flock of strange, birdlike things
Called kweeks, with huge beaks and undersized wings.
With no wild beasts living there to endanger the kweeks,
Their only problem was eating, just filling their beaks.

The kweeks couldn't fly, so they couldn't go anywhere.
Their only food was the tropical fruit growing there:
The purple, pumpkin-sized fruit called a ploppolop
That grew in one towering ploppa treetop.
And since the kweeks were entirely too clumsy to climb,
Getting something to eat was a matter of time.
They often spent hours just waiting around
For the fruit to ripen and fall to the ground.

When the ploppolops ripened and did finally fall,
It was every bird for himself in a wild free-for-all.
Kweek against kweek, with not a one playing fair,

And everyone out to get more than his share.
The rougher and tougher and quicker the kweek,
The more ploppolops he could snatch in his beak.

At nighttime the kweeks were all huddled together
In a cavern for shelter from the foggy, damp weather.
As they slept, the kweeks dreamed the same dream every night,
That they had sprouted huge wings and were on a long flight

To a beautiful island with plenty of space
And ploppa trees growing all over the place.
As they awoke from the dream, they were irked as could be,
When they remembered they had only one ploppa tree.

A kweek named Quentin was so worried one morning,
He made a short speech, which was more of a warning.
"I'm sorry if I sound awfully preachy," he said,
"But if we go on being greedy there's trouble ahead.
When it comes to eating we must try to be fair,
And be sure that no one gets more than his share."
"Terrific! Just dandy!" the kweeks all agreed.
"From now on we'll be fair! Yes! Yes, indeed!"

They tried to think of a plan that was just about right,
So that each kweek got a ploppolop without having to fight.
But some days the ploppolops that dropped from the tree
Might be one hundred, or just two or three.

It was impossible to divide up an uncertain amount,
Especially since the kweeks never learned how to count.
"How many for each?" remained a big question.
Not even Quentin had a suggestion.

The next morning the kweeks were brawling once more,
In a battle of beaks the same as before.
And as Quentin predicted, there was trouble ahead,

And the big troublemaker was a kweek known as Jed.
Every day he out-fought and out-ate everyone,
And in just a few months, he weighed almost a ton.

Jed was selfish and greedy, and not only that:
The big, oversized brute was as quick as a cat.
When a ploppolop dropped, he was ready to pounce
And snap it up in his beak on the very first bounce.
Unless a ploppolop came bouncing their way,
All the rest of the kweeks went hungry all day.

Their bellies had shrunk, with so little to eat.
The kweeks weren't much more than big beaks and big feet.
"We're done for," said Quentin one afternoon,
"Unless we do something drastic real soon.

We can sneak up on Jed before he suspects,
And clobber the brute with a few thousand pecks."
"A dandy idea!" exclaimed the kweeks all at once.
"We'll teach Jed not to bully us poor little runts!"

At twilight when fog drifted in from the sea,
And Jed was napping under the tall ploppa tree,
The whole flock of kweeks, crouching low to the ground,

Crept up to big Jed without making a sound.

"Now remember," warned Quentin, "there's no turning back.

Let's demolish the brute with an all-out attack."

Quentin led the attack, catching Jed by surprise,
With a ferocious peck between his squinty, mean eyes.
But one peck was all, alas and alack.
His friends were too scared to join in the attack.
All at once Quentin found himself beak to beak
With a fighting mad furious gigantic kweek!

"You little creep!" squawked Jed. "You little upstart!
Just for that silly trick, I'm gonna peck you apart!"
Then before he could snatch the small kweek in his beak,
Quentin was gone. He took off like a streak.

The chase was now on, with Jed in red-hot pursuit,
And Quentin zigzagging to escape the big brute.
But the island was such a very small place,
There wasn't much room for a very long chase.

Jed was out to get even, no matter what,
And he finally chased Quentin to a very tight spot
At the edge of a bluff, with nowhere to go,
Unless he jumped into the rough sea down below.
But if he jumped in the sea, he'd be a goner for sure,
And a fierce peck on the head was too much to endure.
There was just one thing left for poor Quentin to do…

In desperation, the little kweek finally flew!
Frantically flapping his wings, he sailed over the head
Of the flabbergasted, befuddled, dumbfounded Jed.
Then out over the island, Quentin went gliding
To surprise his kweek friends, who were all still in hiding.

"Come on out!" Quentin shouted. "Look up here in the sky!
Look at me! I can fly! It's easy as pie!
Now, come on, everyone! Flap your wings and just try it!
We're all light as a feather from our starvation diet!"

And with squeals of delight, the kweeks took off together,
As easy as pie, and as light as a feather.
Then after saying good-bye to Kookatumdee,
The kweeks flew on across the Tumbuzzaroo sea.

And they happened onto an island, as it turned out,
Which resembled the place they had all dreamed about,
With dozens of tall ploppa trees growing there,
And ploppolops for all, with plenty to spare.
They didn't dare overeat, for fear they'd get fat.
The happy kweeks enjoyed flying too much for that.